PENNY AND RIO

The Locked
Doghouse Mystery

Written by Jennifer Swanson
Illustrated by Swapan Debnath

Happy Reading!! :) Jennifer Swanson

ISBN   978-1-936046-10-2
1-936046-10-5

Library of Congress Control Number:
2009903651

Published by Mirror Publishing
Milwaukee, WI 53214

Printed in the USA.

To my parents, who always told me I
could do anything.

Penny and Rio were two lovable dogs who
brought my family great joy in their long and
happy lifetime. They were very much like the
characters in my book.

Jennifer Swanson

"Penny and Rio, the lovable sibling sleuths are off on a backyard adventure with a new friend, Hobbes, the great Dane, to solve a mystery for the anxious mouse, Squeaky, who implores the dogs to retrieve an important treasure before it's too late. Figuring out how to get to the treasure is not easy, especially with the sister dogs snapping insults at each other. What is the treasure? No one but Squeaky knows, and he's not telling. By lending the worried mouse their helping paws, Penny and Rio discover that Squeaky's important treasure is something that's just as important to them. In this heartwarming tale, Swanson creates an entertaining plot with a well-developed cast of characters for independent readers, both boys and girls, who love mystery, adventure, and hanging out with friends."
— *Clara Gillow Clark,* author of *Secrets of Greymoor* Candlewick Press

"Penny and Rio are canine detectives that young readers will love! Their antics are both brave and endearing as they help their friend, Squeaky the mouse. Lots of action and dialogue makes Penny and Rio a good choice for a read aloud."

Barbara Bietz, author of *Like a Maccabee* (Yaldah 2006)

"Penny drags Rio into solving the latest mystery and once again they steal the reader's heart with their charm and personality. Funning, endearing and engaging, I would encourage your early readers (1st and 2nd grade) to try reading this with your help. How can you not get hooked on reading with Penny & Rio? I just can't get enough of Penny & Rio!"

Lisa Barker, Jelly Mom Children's Book Reviews

"Penny and Rio find themselves paw deep in their latest mystery when Hobbes, a huge Great Dane and new next door neighbor seeks them out for their expert detective skills...

Up against an impossible deadline of less than a day, the cleverness of each is put to the test while on the case of finding the lost key. Will they make it in time? Ms. Swanson brings to life the adventures of Penny and Rio with such humanistic characteristics the reader forgets they are on a journey with animals. Children will certainly enjoy reading about the detective skills of such ingenious dogs."

Donna McDine, Write What Inspires You Book Reviews

Chapter One

A New Task

Penny ran around the yard for the third time. "Have you seen that mouse? He was over here by this hole." She looked at Rio. "Are you still mad at me?" Penny asked.

Rio grunted and turned her head.

"I'm sorry I ate your bone last night. You were sleeping. I didn't think you'd mind."

"Hmph!" Rio glared at her.

Penny rolled her eyes.

"Hey, does this hole look bigger to you?"

Sniff! Sniff!

She pushed her nose inside…

Woof!

Penny jumped back. A large brown snout came through the hole.

Sniff! Sniff!

The nose backed out of the hole.

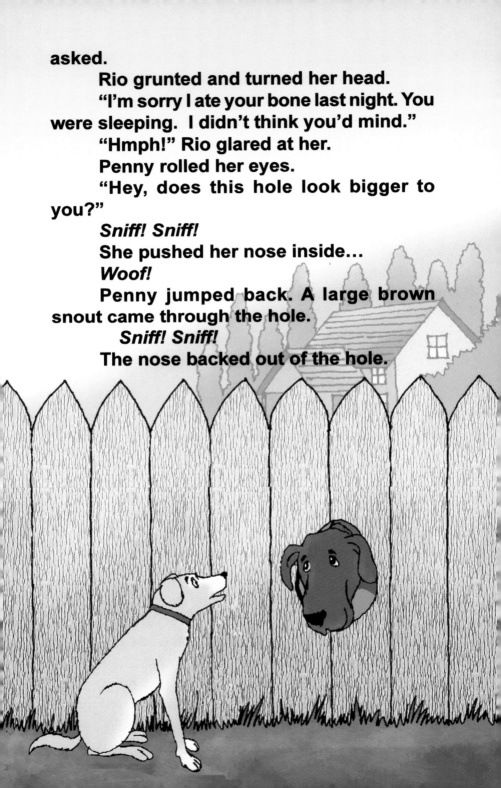

Whump! The whole fence shook, two large paws rested on top. A big brown dog peered down at Penny.

"Who are you?" asked Penny.

"I'm Hobbes."

"I've never see you before. Are you new?" She stepped back to see the dog better.

"Just moved in yesterday," said Hobbes.

"Welcome to the neighborhood." Penny grinned, her tongue hung out, and she showed all her teeth.

"Are you Penny, the detective?" asked Hobbes.

"Yes…"

"There's a mouse here that wants to talk to you." Hobbes called over his shoulder, "Come out, Squeaky. She's here."

A gray mouse cautiously poked his head through the hole.

"H-hi," the mouse trembled. He had long whiskers and a black nose that twitched a lot. "Eek!" Squeaky ran back through the hole.

"What's wrong with him?" Penny said.

"There's a cat over there," Squeaky said in a shaky voice.

"What cat?" Penny looked behind her.

"Th-that cat on your deck," whimpered

Squeaky.

"That's not a cat," Penny laughed. "That's my sister, Rio. What can I do for you?"

"I need your help to get into the old doghouse over here. It's locked," said Squeaky.

"So? Can't you chew a hole in the side of the dog house?"

"He tried that," said Hobbes. "The wood made him sick."

"What's so important?" Penny asked.

Squeaky looked at the ground. "Just some stuff…"

"He wouldn't tell me either," said Hobbes. The fence shook again as he shifted his paws.

"Okay Squeaky, you don't have to tell me," said Penny. "But why is it locked in the doghouse?"

"The dog who owned the house, Spike, used to let me live with him."

"You lived with a dog?"

"Yes, he was nice, and kind of lonely." Squeaky smiled. "Anyway, about two months ago, I went to visit my aunt. When I got back, Spike was gone and the doghouse was locked."

"But why lock that old thing?" said Penny. "No one would want it."

"I know. It's old. There's even a hole in the bottom." Squeaky shrugged. "I guess Spike's owner didn't want anyone to use it."

"Well, I'm not sure I can help. I can't open a metal lock."

"I knew it," Squeaky put his hands over his eyes. "It's gone forever!" He began to cry.

Chapter Two

The Missing Key

     "Don't do that, Squeaky." Penny nudged him with her nose. **"Maybe I can think of something."**
     Squeaky sniffed loudly.

Hobbes rolled his eyes and looked down at Penny. "He does that a lot. He's been crying since I met him."

Penny nodded.

"Where's the key?" Called a voice from the deck.

Penny looked at Rio. "I thought you weren't talking to me."

Rio made a face at Penny and walked down the stairs. Squeaky trembled and backed up when Rio sat next to Penny.

"What did you say?" asked Hobbes.

"I said, where's the key? Every lock has a key."

"Yes, there was a key. Spike hid it in a

bone," Squeaky said.

"Great!" exclaimed Penny. "Where is it?"

"We-ll, it's not that easy." Squeaky looked down at his paws.

"Why?" asked Penny.

"He doesn't know where the key is hidden," said Hobbes.

"You see," explained Squeaky. "Spike and the old dog in your yard sometimes swapped bones. It could be in either yard."

"Oh," said Penny.

"I can understand wanting to hide a bone," mumbled Rio.

"Be quiet, Rio." Penny frowned. "Did Spike give you any clues where he may have hidden the bone?"

"I've got it!" Squeaky jumped to his feet. "Spike said it was hidden near a small tree. Maybe that one over there?" Squeaky pointed to a newly planted tree.

"It's worth a try," said Penny. She looked at Rio, "Are you going to help?"

"No," Rio said lazily, "I think I'll just watch. Besides, digging gets my nails dirty." She smiled and put her head on her paws.

Penny rolled her eyes. "Fine, I'll just dig by myself." Penny walked over to the tree.

"Hey!" called Hobbes. "What about me? Can I do something?"

"Try digging by those new trees in your

yard. Maybe we'll get lucky," said Penny.

Hobbes grinned and showed all his teeth. It was meant to be a smile, but it was kind of scary on such a big animal.

"Cool! I've always wanted to be a detective!" He pulled both of his paws off the fence at the same time.

Cre-eak! The fence swayed in his direction, almost as if it would fall over.

THUMP! It stood upright again.

"That is one BIG dog!" Penny shook her head. She ran to the small tree and started to dig. Dirt flew everywhere. After ten minutes, she had a pretty big hole. It was two feet deep and big enough for her to lie in. She stopped and sat on her back legs, breathing heavily.

"See," said Rio. "I knew it. That's too much exercise for me."

"Walking around the yard is too much exercise for you, Rio," said Penny. She turned to Squeaky, "The bone isn't here. Where else should we look?"

"Gosh, I don't know." Squeaky looked around the yard. "Maybe he hid it behind a bush?"

"A bush? But there are tons of them!" Penny looked at the bushes that bordered the yard.

"Sorry," Squeaky shrugged.

Penny sighed. There were probably

fifteen bushes in the yard.

"It won't be that bad," said Rio. "I bet you don't have to dig deep to find the bone. Not everyone digs big holes like you do," she teased.

"Does that mean you're going to help?" asked Penny.

"Nope."

"Come on, Rio, I'll let you have my bone tonight." Penny smiled.

Rio stopped. Her eyes narrowed. "Say it's for the next two nights, and you've got a deal."

"Okay, you win." Penny smiled.

Rio licked her lips.

"You start with these bushes. I'll go to the other side of the yard and get those. We'll meet in the middle."

Rio walked to the nearest bush and began to dig, very slowly.

"What can I do?" asked Squeaky.

"Go check on Hobbes. Let me know if you find anything," said Penny. She turned and ran to the far side of the yard.

Squeaky crawled through the hole.

Splat! A pile of dirt hit Squeaky in the face.

"I've got something!" Hobbes yelled.

Squeaky wiped his eyes and looked. Hobbes was proudly holding a plastic steak in his mouth.

"No, that's not it," said Squeaky.

Hobbes spit out the steak, shrugged, and kept digging.

"Hey, I've got it!" shouted Penny.

Squeaky ran over to see.

Penny held up a rawhide bone covered in dirt. "Squeaky, clean it out. See if the key's inside."

Squeaky quickly dug through the dirt caked inside of the bone.

"Nothing," he said. He put his head down.

"Over here," called Rio. She had dug up two bones and three tennis balls. Squeaky quickly emptied the bones of dirt.

"Nothing, again," he said.

And so it went. Each dog found bones where they were digging. None of them was the bone with the key in it. At the end of the day, a tired Penny and Rio met Hobbes and Squeaky at the fence.

"Well, we've found enough bones, tennis balls, and plastic toys to play with for the next two years," said Penny.

"But no key." Squeaky sniffed.

"I'm beat." Penny looked at Rio, asleep on the ground.

"Me too," said Hobbes. He yawned, then stretched out in the grass.

"Don't give up hope, Squeaky, we'll think of something." Penny closed her eyes and went to sleep, dreaming of bushes and a big bone with a key in it.

Squeaky, too sad to sleep, chewed on the fence hole.

Chapter Three

Forcing The Lock

The next morning, Penny woke up, ready to go. "Hey, Squeaky!" she called. "I've got a plan." Squeaky ran through the hole in the fence that was much bigger now.

"Nice job on the hole."

"Thanks, Penny," Squeaky smiled. "What's the plan?"

"We need Hobbes. Is he awake?" asked Penny.

Squeaky nodded, "He can't wait to be a detective."

"Great," said Rio. "Not another one!" She put her head on her paws and sighed.

Penny grinned. "Hey Hobbes, come here. I've got a plan."

Hobbes bounded to the fence.

Thump!

The fence hit Penny in the head.

"Ouch! Take it easy, Hobbes."

Hobbes bent down and thrust his head through the hole. "Sorry, Penny. So, what's up?"

"Since we can't find the key, we could force the lock off with something."

"Hmm," said Hobbes, "that might work. But what?"

"That," she said. Penny pointed to the new tree she'd dug around yesterday.

"But that tree is in the ground," said Squeaky.

"I'll gnaw it off." Penny grinned.

"What? You're going to chew off a tree?" Rio shook her head. "Leave me out of this." She sighed and rolled over.

"What can I do? I want to be a detective,

too," said Hobbes.

"You will. You get to use the tree to open the lock," said Penny. "Squeaky can help."

"Great!" Squeaky nodded. "Anything to get my stuff back."

"But what can I do now?" asked Hobbes.

"Try breaking the lock," said Penny.

"Great idea!" Hobbes pulled his big head out of the hole and ran to the doghouse.

Penny looked at Rio, asleep on the deck, again, and snoring very loudly.

"Hmph!" Penny snorted. "I need a new side-kick. One that likes to work more than sleep!" Shaking her head, Penny ran to the tree.

"Penny!" Squeaky called. "Do you want some help? I'm feeling much better."

"Sure, can you make the hole in the fence bigger?" asked Penny.

"No problem," said Squeaky. He sat next to the fence and began chewing.

Penny took the first bite of the tree and spit it out.

"Yuck! I wonder if this tree will make me sick?" she mumbled. She took a deep breath then started chewing on the trunk.

Forty-five minutes later, the small tree crashed to the ground with a bounce.

"Timber!" Rio called. She rolled to her feet and plodded to the end of the deck. "You are in trouble now."

Penny made a face at her then called to Squeaky. "The tree is down. Are you ready for me?"

"Sure!" Squeaky called back. He stepped away from the hole. "You won't have any trouble pushing the tree through now."

Penny put her head through the fence. "Hobbes, we need your help!"

Hobbes ran over. "Sorry, I couldn't get the lock off."

"That's okay," said Penny. "This should work. Let me drag the tree over." Penny ran to the fallen tree. Even though it was small, it was pretty long. It had to be over six feet in length.

Penny grabbed the tree with her teeth, dug her back paws into the ground, and heaved with all her might. The tree moved a little. She bit down and pulled again. The leaves on the top branches dragged against the grass. It took a long time to pull it across the yard.

"Ha! Ha! That looks like fun." Rio laughed from the deck.

"You could help, you useless dog," Penny muttered through the tree in her mouth.

"You're doing just fine, Penny." Rio giggled. She shook with laughter.

Hobbes watched from the fence hole. "That's a pretty big tree, Penny. What am I supposed to do with it?"

"You're going to use the tree to force open the lock," explained Penny.

Hobbes frowned. "How am I going to do that?"

"Don't worry, I'll show you," Penny said. "Grab the end of the tree as I push it through to you."

Hobbes clamped his teeth on the small tree. He pulled with all his might.

Bam! Penny's head bounced off the fence.

"Hey, be careful!" Penny yelled. "That was my head!"

"Sorry," He muttered. Hobbes closed his teeth around the tree, leaned back on his paws, and pulled.

Thud! The tree flew into the yard.

Penny looked through the fence. "Great job, Hobbes! Now we can break open the lock."

"Uh-oh, we have a problem," said Hobbes. "The doghouse is only three feet tall, and the tree is twice as long. How is the tree going to fit under the lock to break it off?"

25

Penny looked at the tree, then at the doghouse. "You're right," she said. She flopped down and put her head on her paws.

"Now what do we do?" Squeaky began to sniffle.

Rio walked over from the deck and looked at the tree lying on the ground. "Great going Penny!" she laughed.

"Quiet, Rio," Penny muttered.

"I have an idea. . ." began Rio.

"I don't want to hear it," said Penny. "You've been against this from the start. All you do is laugh and make fun. Now leave me alone while I figure out what to do."

"Fine," Rio grumbled, "suit yourself." She plopped down on the ground and promptly went to sleep.

Chapter Four

Project Tip Over

An hour later, Penny still didn't have a plan.

"Are you ready to hear my idea?" Rio rolled over and walked to the edge of the deck.

"I'm listening," Penny sighed.

"Have Squeaky chew off the bottom and all the branches to make a 'Y' shape. Fit the 'Y' under the lock. Then Hobbes can push down on the branch and pop the lock." Rio grinned.

"Hmmm, it might work." Penny smiled. "Thanks, Rio. Squeaky… "

"I'm going," he cried. Squeaky raced to the tree. He chewed and chewed.

A few minutes later, Hobbes pushed the 'Y' of the tree under the lock.

"Whenever you're ready," Penny said.

Hobbes stepped onto the bottom of the tree with his front paw. The tree bowed upward. It pushed the lock away from the doghouse.

Hobbes pushed harder. The lock stood out straight from the doghouse.

Hobbes kept pushing. The lock strained against the latch.

"Look out Squeaky!" Penny yelled.

Crack!

The tree broke in half! Part of it flew through the air. The other half fell to the ground. The lock was slowly swinging back and forth against the doghouse. It made a slight thumping sound.

"It didn't work!" Squeaky whimpered. "I'll never get my treasure!" He put his head in his hands and cried.

"Don't lose hope, Squeaky." Penny said.

"Hobbes! Hobbes! Come here, boy!" Hobbes' owner called from the back door. Penny pulled her head out of the fence hole so the man wouldn't see her.

Hobbes' owner came out on the deck. "Hobbes, what are you doing?" Hobbes was standing next to the doghouse. "Is that old doghouse still bothering you, boy? Well, don't worry, it'll be gone tomorrow. I'm taking it to the dump the first thing in the morning. I'll get you a brand new one. Come on inside."

The owner motioned with his hand. Hobbes looked sadly at Penny and slowly followed his owner inside.

Squeaky crept out from behind the doghouse. "We're doomed," he said.

"We can still look for the key," Penny said.

"But you heard Hobbes' owner, he's getting rid of the doghouse tomorrow morning. We'll never find the key by then." Squeaky put his head in his hands again. His shoulders shook with tears.

"Don't cry, Squeaky," said Penny.

"We'll figure it out."

"Squeaky," Rio interrupted, "is your stuff breakable?"

"What?" Squeaky stopped crying and looked at Rio.

"I said, is it breakable?"

"No."

"Then why can't we just tip the doghouse over? Didn't you say that there was a big hole in the bottom of it?"

"Yes... Why didn't I think of it before? That's a great idea, Rio!" Squeaky said, hopeful again.

Penny looked doubtfully at Rio and then the doghouse. "How are we going to do that?"

"We'll get Hobbes to help," replied Rio.

Penny stuck her head through the hole and peered around the bush at Hobbes' back door. "He's got to come out first."

"We have work to do before he does," said Rio. She pawed at the ground. "Start digging, Penny. We need to dig under the fence so we can get through to Hobbes' yard."

Penny frowned. "It'll never work," she grumbled. But, she began to dig with Rio.

Squeaky stepped back from the flying dirt and clasped his hands together. "I hope this works, I hope this works," he said over and over.

A short time later, Rio stopped digging. "Okay, Penny, I think we can fit through now."

"Not bad," said Penny, "and since it's hidden by this bush, I don't think our owner will notice it. Well, maybe not."

Just then, Hobbes ran out the back door. "Do you have a new plan?" he asked.

"Yep," said Penny. "Rio thought of it. She says that we should tip the doghouse over so that Squeaky can climb in and get his stuff."

Hobbes looked at the doghouse and then shrugged. "Why not? Let's try it. Come on over, I'm going to need help with this."

Penny and Rio squeezed under the fence. Then all three dogs pressed their front paws against the side of the doghouse.

"On the count of three," said Penny. "One, two, THREE!" They pushed as hard as they could. The doghouse didn't move.

They pushed again.

Slowly the doghouse lifted off the ground.

Squeaky jumped up and down. "It's working!" he shouted.

"Uggghhh!" Rio grunted as she leaned into the doghouse with all her might..

Crash! Boom!

The doghouse flipped onto its side.

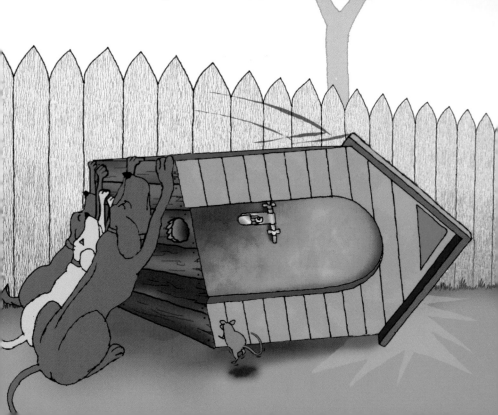

"You did it!" Squeaky yelled. He ran to the doghouse and scrambled up the side to the hole. With a big grin at his friends, he climbed inside.

"Maybe now we'll get to see what was so important," Rio said.

Hobbes, panting, sat down hard on the ground. "Yeah, and I hope it was worth all this effort." Hobbes motioned towards the doghouse with his head. "He's back."

Squeaky climbed out of the doghouse carrying a large red bag over his shoulder. He was beaming.

"Thanks for the help, guys," said Squeaky. He slid down the side of the doghouse and hurried towards the hole in the fence.

Chapter Five

Treasure

"Hey, wait a minute!" Penny called. "Aren't you going to show us what was so important?"

Squeaky stopped and put his head

down. "You'll think it's silly."

"No we won't. We promise," said Penny. Hobbes and Rio nodded.

"Okay," Squeaky said. He slid the bag off his back. He reached inside, and pulled out a well-worn green book, and set it on the ground. Next, he pulled out a new blue book and set it on top of the green one. "Well, here they are." Squeaky smiled proudly.

Rio snorted. "We went through all of this for some old books?"

"Not just any books," Squeaky flushed. "They're my family photo albums. They mean a lot to me. I have the only copies and they've been in my family for years." He looked at the disappointed faces on the dogs. "See, I knew you'd think it was silly."

"Squeaky, if they were important to you, then it was worth it," said Penny. "We were happy to help." She smiled.

Squeaky grinned. He put the books carefully back into the bag.

"But don't we get to see them?" asked Hobbes. "We worked pretty hard to get them."

Squeaky looked at the three dogs. "Do you really want to see?"

Rio shrugged. "Sure, why not? I've never seen mice pictures, before."

"We-l-l-l, all right," said Squeaky. He put the bag on the ground again and took out the green book. "I love to show them off," he grinned.

Penny walked over to Squeaky and flopped on the ground. Rio lay down next to her. Hobbes stood over the two dogs, and lowered his massive head to see better.

Squeaky opened the green book. The first picture was of a mouse with an old sailing hat. "That's my great-great grandfather, Isaac. He was a ship captain," Squeaky said proudly.

"A mouse was a captain of a ship?" asked Rio. "Must have been a pretty small ship," she chuckled.

As Squeaky turned the pages, the dogs

looked at the pictures inside. Some of the mice in the photos had on very old dresses with grim expressions on their faces. Others were children, dressed in their very best clothes and looking as if they were frozen in place. Towards the end of the book, the mice were in newer clothing. They even looked happy.

Page by page, Squeaky explained who they were. "Here's my great-grandmother; she had twelve kids. One of her children, Todd, was a famous baker. He was known for baking the best cheese sandwich in the whole county. That's my great-uncle Sam. He drove a tank in the army…"

Penny raised her eyebrows
and looked at Rio over Squeaky's head.
Rio rolled her eyes. Squeaky kept talking,
proudly showing off his family.

"What's in the other book?" Rio asked.

"That book has my family in it."
Squeaky put down the green book. He
opened the blue one. The first picture was
of two mice. The male mouse was dressed
in gray pants and a blue sweater. The female
mouse was dressed in a pale blue dress.
"Those are my parents," Squeaky said
proudly. He looked at the dogs expectantly.

"They look nice," said Hobbes.
Squeaky smiled.

40

The first few pages were covered with smaller mice, all smiling and looking very happy. "These are my brothers and sisters." He turned the next page and it was blank.

"Thank goodness!" whispered Rio.

"Did you say something?" Squeaky asked.

"I was just wondering why those pages are blank?" asked Rio.

"They're for when my brothers and sisters and I have kids," answered Squeaky.

"Family must be very important to you, Squeaky," said Penny.

"Oh, it is," Squeaky replied as he closed the book. "Family is the most important treasure of all."

Penny looked at Rio. "I guess that means we should appreciate each other, huh?"

"I guess so," Rio nodded. She turned to Squeaky. "You know, you're right, Squeaky, family is important, especially when they can get you extra bones," she grinned.

Penny laughed.

Squeaky picked up both books and put them back in the sack.

"So," asked Penny, "what are you going to do now?" The three dogs stood up and looked at Squeaky.

"I thought I'd go live with my mom for a while," said Squeaky. "She has a nice

41

place."

"Time for me to go." He picked up the heavy sack and threw it over his shoulder. Squeaky headed for the front gate. He raised his hand and waved. "Bye!" He headed for the front gate.

"We have to go, too," said Penny. "See ya', Hobbes."

Penny and Rio squeezed back through the fence.

"Hey, Rio, we'd better fill in this hole before our owner sees it."

Penny and Rio worked together to fill in the hole. When they were done, they climbed on the deck and lay down.

"Well, that's over. It was fun, though wasn't it, Rio? Rio?" Penny looked at Rio. She was stretched out on the deck snoring softly.

"Asleep already?" Penny said. "Well, it has been a long day. I wonder if we'll find a new adventure tomorrow?" Penny closed her eyes and went to sleep.

Little did Penny know that her new adventure was just outside her front gate.

LaVergne, TN USA
29 August 2010
194951LV00001B

9 781936 046102